The True Story of George

Ingrid Lee

with illustrations by
Stéphane Denis

ORCA BOOK PUBLISHERS

National Library of Canada Cataloguing in Publication Data:

Lee, Ingrid, 1948-

The true story of George / Ingrid Lee ; with illustrations

by Stéphane Denis.

(Orca echoes)

ISBN 1-55143-293-5

I. Denis, Stephané, 1971- II. Title. III. Series.

PS8623.E44T78 2004   jC813'.6   C2004-903835-4

Library of Congress Control Number: 2004108985

Summary: Two children find a small plastic toy man who fancies himself a hero.

Orca Book Publishers gratefully acknowledges the support for its
publishing programs provided by the following agencies:
the Government of Canada through the Department of Canadian Heritage's
Book Publishing Industry Development Program (BPIDP),
the Canada Council for the Arts, and the British Columbia Arts Council.

Design and typesetting by Lynn O'Rourke

Orca Book Publishers
1016 Balmoral Road
Victoria, BC Canada
V8T 1A8

Orca Book Publishers
PO Box 468
Custer, WA USA
98240-0468

Printed and bound in Canada
on Old Growth Forest Free, 100% Recycled paper.
07 06 05 04 • 4 3 2 1

To Katie and Mackenzie.

George
Catches a Wave

Up! Up! He climbed through the sky on a wave of white water. The wave licked the big sky like a giant tongue. It was the greatest wave in the sea and he, George the Brave, George the Steadfast, rode the wild thing.

The spray soaked his hair. The light of the sun dazzled his eyes. But George stayed on top. He soared above the earth. Higher than a gull. Higher than a jet plane. Higher than the moon!

Down. The giant wave collapsed under him. The sea opened its big mouth and sucked the water back. George fell through the hole, down, down, until the water swallowed him with a great gulp.

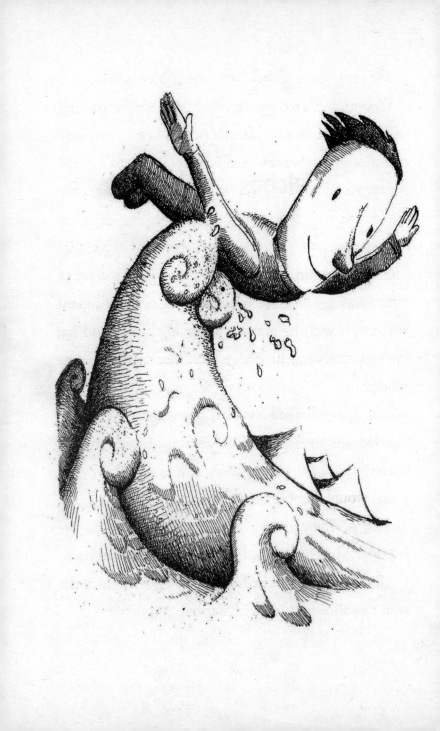

He sank like a stone into a deep blue world.

George gathered his strength. He was not going to be a shark snack. He swung his arms, first one and then the other. He was a red-ribbon champion, coming up from his dive, cutting through the water like a speeding bullet. The roar of the sea cheered him on as he shot out of the water and into the air.

Water crashed about him, tossing him back and forth as if he were a basketball. The waves slam-dunked him again and again. Each time, George surfaced, moving his arms, first one and then the other.

Let the water do its best. He was George the Brave, George the Steadfast. He would catch another wave to the top.

He would conquer the ocean!

Katie and Mackenzie
See Red

"What's that?"

Something bright red bobbled at the edge of the beach. Katie scooped it from the water and showed it to her brother.

"Look what I found."

Mackenzie stared at the thing in her hand. It wasn't fancy. It wasn't a T-Rex with multiple brains or a glow bug from Uranus. It didn't have any bells and whistles or lights and beepers. It was just a little guy made out of plastic.

"Let me see him," Mackenzie said.

"Just a minute!" Katie took a closer look at the toy. The little guy had black hair and pale skin, and he wore a red jumpsuit and red shoes. He wasn't as big as her hand. He wasn't much bigger than her middle finger.

She twisted the parts. The legs moved. They were joined together so when one went up, the other did too. The arms moved one at a time though. And the head twisted.

Katie turned the head around and around as if she were screwing on the lid of a jam jar. "I wonder what he's supposed to do," she said.

Then she gave him to her brother.

In the car on the way home, Mackenzie tried to pull off the head, but it was too small and slippery. He couldn't think of anything else to do with the toy. He decided it wasn't much good. After a while he threw it on the floor in the backseat.

The little guy landed between a plastic container of window washer fluid and a piece of string. He stayed there for a long time.

George
Escapes

George was in a fight for his life! The octopus wrapped around him, trying to tear his body apart, limb from limb.

He pretended he was dead. He kept his mouth shut. But he didn't close his eyes. He was George the Brave, George the Steadfast.

The mollusc squeezed his chest. The long tentacles tried to pull him right out of his jumpsuit. They tried to steal his shoes.

Two of the tentacles bent his legs. They yanked his arms until one almost came right out of its socket. Then they tried to take his head!

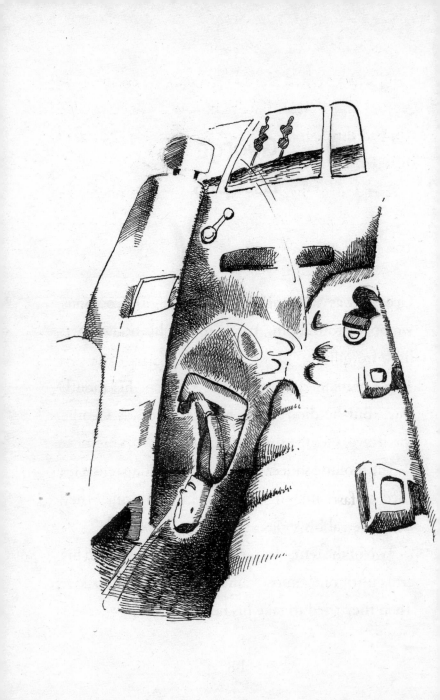

George waited for a chance to escape. He waited and waited. Finally he saw an opening. He slipped through the arms of the beast like a greased banana.

Head over heels he cartwheeled through the air. He executed his final move in the gymnastics competition. He was smooth. He was graceful. He was an Olympian!

Whump! With a triple back-flip finish he landed on the mat. The crowd roared. He took the gold!

After all that he was just a bit dizzy. His ears hummed. The clouds in the sky whirled and swirled and twirled. He decided to stretch out and relax.

George liked the sound in his ears. It was not too loud and not too soft, not too high and not too low, not too fast and not too slow. He liked the soft mat underneath him. The air felt fresh and clean.

He fell asleep.

Katie and Mackenzie Go Fishing

School was over for the day. Katie and Mackenzie went home in the back of the car. Mackenzie kicked at the container of window wash. He saw the little red figure on the floor. "Hey," he said. "Here's that little guy."

"He's mine," said Katie. "I found him at the beach."

"You can have him," said Mackenzie. "He doesn't do anything. He doesn't even have any weapons. You can't take anything off or put anything on."

Katie looked at the container of window wash on the floor of the car. "Let's dunk him in there," she said. It was a strange thing to say. Why would she think of doing that? But she did.

She reached down and pulled up the window wash and took off the lid.

"Yeah!" said Mackenzie. He thought that was a good idea too. He was surprised. Sisters don't usually come up with good ideas. But this time he couldn't deny it. "There's some string here too," he said. "Tie him on one end. You can hold the other. Then we can get him out."

They wrapped the string around the little figure and lowered him into the soap. He looked like a fish on a line.

They swished him around. Then they pulled him out. Then they dunked him again. Then they pulled him out. They did this over and over. It got kind of boring.

Finally they let the string fall in the window wash. The little guy landed on the bottom of the container and Mackenzie snapped on the lid.

"Shake it up," said Katie.

Mackenzie shook the container. The blue soap sloshed around until pretty soon all you could see were bubbles. You could hardly see the figure. You couldn't see his head or his shoes. All you could see was a bit of the red jumpsuit.

The car pulled into the driveway. Katie and her brother went inside the house for dinner.

They left the little plastic figure in the container of window washer fluid.

George,
Roped and Soaped

George woke up. The humming had stopped. He was all wet. The world was filled with suds. Bubbles popped around him like glass balloons.

He tried to stand, but he was all tied up! How could he wash his face if he was all tied up?

George tried not to blink. He drew in his breath as much as he could. He thought small, smaller than a grain of sand, smaller than a speck of dust.

He concentrated on his chest and his arms. He concentrated so much that he grew smaller and the rope grew looser. Then the rope had nothing to hold onto. It slid off George like spaghetti off a fork. He was free. He was the greatest escape artist since Houdini!

Now he could have a bubble bath!

It was the best bath ever. The suds made duckies and frogs and turtles. They made alphabet letters. George found enough shapes to spell his name. All except for the last e.

George let the soap wash his neck and clean out his ears. He let the liquid shine his shoes. His jumpsuit became redder, his hair became blacker and his flesh became pinker.

He was as fresh as a daisy.

He was the cleanest man in the world!

Katie and Mackenzie Play with Parachutes

"What are you making?" asked Katie. Her brother was sitting at the kitchen table.

"A parachute," said Mackenzie. Katie watched as he cut off the handles of a white plastic bag from the dollar store. He poked a hole at the edge of the bag. He poked another and another and another. There were four holes in four different places along the edge.

Mackenzie tied a piece of thread around each hole. The other ends of the thread dangled in space.

"Now I need a passenger," said Mackenzie. "Something not too heavy."

"I know where to get one," said Katie.

She went out to the car and fished the little plastic guy out of the window washer fluid. "You can use this guy," she said.

"Hey," said Mackenzie, "he looks pretty clean." He tied two strings of his parachute to each of the little toy's arms. "Now for a test dive," he said. "Good thing he's got a jumpsuit."

"Give him a name," said Katie.

"Fang," said Mackenzie.

"That's dumb. He's not a snake," said Katie.

"Fungus," said Mackenzie.

"That's worse," said Katie. "He's not a mushroom either. Just call him George."

They threw George off the bed.

Crash!

He nose-dived to the floor. The parachute tangled around his arms and neck and they had to cut the strings and make new ones.

Then they threw him from the top of the stairs.

Thud! Thud! Thud!

George hit three steps on the way down.

"We need to be higher," said Katie. So they climbed up to the top of the house and threw him out their mother's bathroom window.

Whoosh!

A gust of wind grabbed the bag and blew it past the chimney. A crow sitting on the roof saw it. Maybe the crow thought George was a dragonfly. Or maybe it thought George was a giant ladybug. Who knows what it thought?

"Look," yelled Mackenzie. "A crow is attacking my parachute."

The crow snatched the parachute in its claws. The bird hauled the bag and the little figure over the neighbor's roof. When it got to the park with the maple trees it disappeared.

George disappeared too.

"Wow!" said Mackenzie.

"We'll never find him now," said Katie. "George is gone for good."

21

George
Jumps

After his bath, George had a surprise. His parachute was ready! He was going to sky-dive. He would jump solo!

A giant crane hauled him into the air. George gave the operator a wave. The crane let him go.

Crash!

The ground came up so fast it smacked his bum. George tried to stand. He was caught in the cords. He twisted this way and that. Finally he was free.

He needed new cords. He needed more sky. He needed another chance!

He would try again. Everybody knows that if you don't get it right the first time, you have to try, try, try again.

Thud! Thud! Thud!

George bounced all the way down the hill like a bottle cap. It was a good hill. It was covered in soft grass. But it was not high enough to fill his chute full of air. He had to find the highest peak ever. He had to pick a spot so high that fences would look like toothpicks and cars would look like dinky toys. He needed a sky-high, free-fall, deep-drop zone.

He would try again!

George launched himself into the sky! He stretched out his arms and felt the air rush by his face. He heard the crackle when the parachute caught its breath and spread its wings. Then the ropes gave a yank.

George stopped his free-fall. He sailed through the air like a leaf in the fall, like a feather in the breeze, like a ticket in the subway.

He surfed the currents of wind. He swung away from the peaks of the mountain ranges that blocked his way. They were too steep and too hard. He wanted to land in a patch of green, not on a piece of slate.

But there was trouble in the breezes. A giant crow, black as ink, swooped out of nowhere, its iron beak aimed straight for George's heart!

George jumped into action. He caught a downdraft and swept under the bird. He was just in time. The beak snapped on empty air. But the claws of the crow snagged the parachute.

The crow headed for the mountains with George in its clutches. He was heading for the rocks! He might tear his jumpsuit. He might scuff his shoes. There was no time to lose.

George looked down. A soft green cloud floated right under him. He raised his arms, abandoned his chute and fell through the sky. The crow didn't even notice he was gone.

The leafy net slowed his fall. Touchdown! He landed in a little house.

It was made of wattle and daub. The spaces between the twigs were packed with clay. What a piece of real estate! Shelter from the rain, a great view and a feather bed. He would buy it. He was George the Brave, George the Steadfast. And now he was George the Property Man!

Katie and Mackenzie Build a Fort

Katie and Mackenzie stood in the middle of the park. It was a cold day in November, the day after the first big snowfall of the season.

"It's packing snow. Let's build a fort under this tree," said Katie. She got down on her hands and knees and began to tunnel into a drift of white stuff.

"I'll start on the other side," Mackenzie said, "and meet you in the middle." He went around the other side and started to scoop snow away too.

"Hey!" he said. "There's something in the tunnel."

Mackenzie dug away the snow. "It's an old nest," he said. "Something's in it." He pulled out a patch of red. "It's George," he yelled. "I found George!"

He backed out of his end of the tunnel and held up the little guy.

Katie backed out of her end of the tunnel and stared at it.

"Now it's mine," Mackenzie said. "I found him this time."

That wasn't very fair. He had thrown George out the window. But he said it anyway.

Katie shook her head. "You made the parachute that got him lost. So we're even. Besides," she added, "he's probably come out of the back end of a crow."

Mackenzie dropped the toy and Katie picked it up.

"He can be the watchman for the fort," she said. "I'll put him up here."

She stuck George into the snow above her hole.

They got back to digging. Soon Katie disappeared into the hill of snow at one end. Mackenzie disappeared into the hill at the other end.

The park looked empty. Nobody walking along would see anybody there. Katie and Mackenzie were under the snow. Nobody would notice the little man in the jumpsuit. He was far too small.

After some more digging, Katie stuck out her hand and it went right through the snowy wall in front of her. It went right through to the other side. Her mitten boffed Mackenzie on the nose.

"Hey!" Mackenzie yelled. He stuck his mitten out in front of him. It went right through the hole to the other side. Katie got snow in her mouth.

Both of them began to push at the snow in front of them. They tried to make the other one back up. They forgot they wanted to build a fort in the middle.

The hill sagged. A big pile of snow fell down Mackenzie's collar. Cold water trickled down his back. He was so surprised that he stood up.

The snow caved in around him.

Katie had to stick out her head to get some air.

The fort lay in ruins around their feet.

"Look what you did, you idiot!" said Katie. She threw some snow at her brother and scrambled out of the wreckage. He scrambled after her, throwing a snowball that whizzed by her ear.

They ran home yelling at each other, making enough noise to wake the worms.

George
Gets Snowed In

Guard of the fort! George stood at attention, his arms at his sides, his back straight, his legs together. He looked neither to the left nor to the right. He was George the Brave, George the Steadfast. He would not move a muscle, not even if the sky fell down.

The snow shifted under his feet. Little pieces of ice rolled over his red shoes. The earth shuddered. It was an avalanche!

Giant cracks split the fort. They were wider than the lines in the sidewalk, wider than the St. Lawrence River, wider than a Martian canal.

Chunks of ice toppled from the crags around him.

George held to his post. He waited to make sure the fort was empty before he saved himself.

It was almost too late. He rolled sideways, this way and that, playing dodgeball with the ice. Finally he ducked into a cave.

Snow covered the entrance. It wasn't a cave anymore. It was a tomb. He was trapped!

It was cold, colder than a refrigerator, colder than the middle of an ice-cream sandwich. Luckily his jumpsuit was a triple-layer thermal one.

George looked at the white walls. He watched the shadows. He saw one shadow that was darker than the other ones. It wasn't a shadow. It wasn't even a wall. There was a tunnel at the back of the cave. A way out!

He would follow that tunnel. He would follow it deep into another world of icicles and pools without bottoms. Maybe he would find the bones of a musk ox. Maybe he would find the Sasquatch! Maybe he would come out on the other side of the world!

Katie
Mails George

Mackenzie was playing baseball in the park when he stepped on something hard. He looked down and there was George. He picked the little toy up. It still had all its parts and so he put it in his pocket.

Later on he gave it to his sister. "Here," he said. "Now I've found George two times. You can have him anyway."

Katie was sending some stamps to a friend. Her friend had the chicken pox and he was working on his stamp collection while he waited to get better.

Nowadays people don't send letters much. They send e-mails. But you can't send stamps by e-mail, and Katie had a stamp of a polar bear and a stamp of the *Bluenose*. The *Bluenose* was a sailing ship. It was a funny name for a ship. The ship on the stamp was blue, so that part was all right. But it didn't have a nose. Most ships don't. Katie wondered who thought of that name.

"He can go for a ride," Katie said. She wrapped a tissue around him so his shoe wouldn't poke a hole in the stamps.

She put him in the envelope and sealed it. She should have waited. It was hard to write the address of her friend on the front. The envelope was bumpy, but she finally got it done. Before she mailed the letter she stuck a stamp with a red maple leaf in the corner. One stamp like that was enough to mail two stamps. Wasn't that odd?

Katie's friend got the letter two days later. He liked the stamps. But he didn't think much of the little guy. You couldn't do anything with him. You couldn't even give him the chicken pox.

He threw George into a box of junk in his closet.

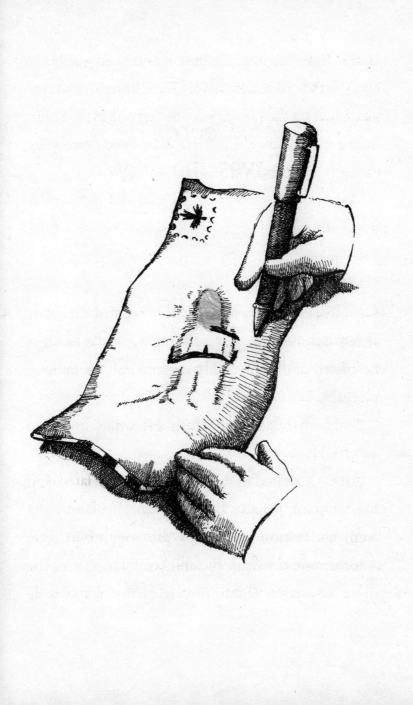

George
Saves the Day

George let the snow melt away. He pulled the white sheets around him and had a nap. While he slept he tossed and turned. He dreamed about faraway places.

Suddenly he felt hot breath. He woke up. It was an attack!

Aliens marched toward him. One of them looked like a potato. It had a big juicy mouth, giant white teeth and a nose that stuck way out of its face. Another one was made of some sort of metal, maybe silver, or maybe aluminum. It carried a molecule shuffler in one hand and a web warp in the other. There was a rubber monster too, with a back full of spines and a belly blotter.

They circled George, coming in closer and closer. He turned around and around to protect his back. He was George the Brave, George the Steadfast. No one was going to make a surprise move on him.

George had no weapons but his quick wits and his strong body.

Aggh! Spines raked his leg. The belly tried to wipe him out! George kicked the monster away. Then the shiny alien struck at George's neck with its molecule shuffler.

George was not going to lose his head. He kept his wits. He ducked.

The potato took the blow on its gigantic red nose. It popped off and hit the alien's arm, the one holding the web warp. The warp got stuck in the spines of the monster with the belly blotter.

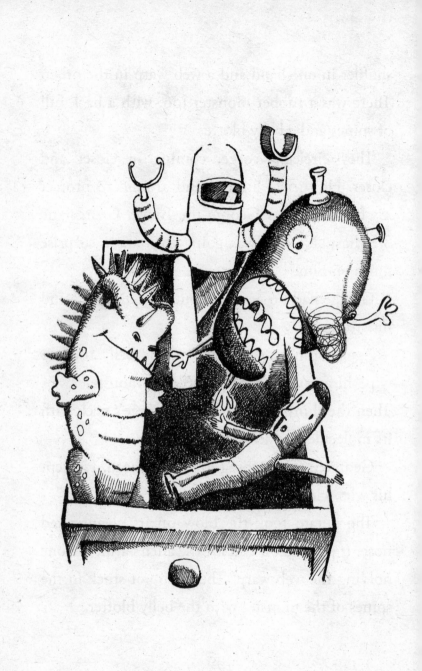

All the aliens began to fight each other. George let them. They would destroy each other. He had saved himself. He had saved the earth. He had saved the universe.

He was a hero!

Katie
at School

When he got better and all the red spots went away, Katie's friend went back to school.

Just before he left his house he looked for something to give Katie from his box of stuff. He found a rubber hedgehog with an eraser on the belly. It was almost new. He thought that would do.

He found George too, so he took the little guy to school as well. Katie could have him back.

Katie liked the hedgehog. But she screwed up her nose when her friend handed back George. She looked at the toy. "He keeps turning up," she said. "I'll put him in my bag. Maybe he can get an education." She shoved him in a pocket so his top

half stuck out of the flap. The bag was black and George was red so he stuck out a lot. He stuck out like a sore thumb.

When she walked down the hall, all of the other kids noticed the little guy.

"Hey, Katie," they teased. "Is that your new boyfriend?"

"It's just George," she said. "He's not mine. He's just a dumb toy. I'm going to give it back to my brother."

But she didn't tuck him away. Everybody could still see him sticking out of a pocket on her schoolbag.

George
at School

George loved school.

In French class he repeated the words over and over in his head. He imagined how they would roll off his tongue if he were a gentleman from Lucerne. *Bonjour, Mademoiselle. Parlez-vous français?* He thought of another phrase. *Avez-vous un peu de beurre?* Soon he would treat himself to a fine French meal in a quaint little restaurant in Quebec. He would have French fries, or maybe French toast. He would wink at the waitress and he would say "*Le chèque, s'il vous plâit!*"

"*Ooh, la la,*" the waitress would reply with a twinkle in her eye.

Mathematics class was a challenge. Two times ten is twenty. Ten times two is twenty. Ten plus ten divided by two times two is twenty. But only sometimes.

George was not going to be fooled. Twenty divided by two was ten! Always. That was logical. George understood logic. He knew if he did the questions over and over he would get them right. That was logical too.

In art the class was studying the figure. They picked George to be the model.

George put up his right arm. He twisted his neck to the side. He put his best foot forward. The other foot went too. Then he stood very still.

The artists crowded around. They tried to draw his long straight nose and his bright blue eyes. They tried to draw the waves in his hair. They tried to draw the smooth curves of his jumpsuit.

Imagine! His picture would be on every fridge in the city!

Later he would stand in front of a mirror. He would draw himself. He would be the artist and he would be the model.

In English class George cried over Casey and his last swing at bat. He laughed at the cat who came out of the hat. He quivered when the raven spoke.

Then he wrote his own poem. He was George the Brave, George the Steadfast. And now he was George the Man of Letters!

George's Poem

I think that I shall never see
A finer sort of guy than me:
So brave, so strong,
So straight and tall,
I am George, the Best of All!

Mackenzie
Builds a Model

Katie and Mackenzie were doing their homework at the kitchen table. Sometimes they did their homework in their bedrooms. But that day they needed a big table.

Mackenzie was making a dinosaur out of green plasticine. He had a shoebox ready for his model. There were green paper leaves all over the inside of the box.

He made a pretty good dinosaur. It had a long tail on one end of a big belly and a long neck on the other end. The neck was so long the head of the dinosaur had to rest on the bottom of the box.

Katie was drawing a picture of a volcano. She looked at her brother's model. "The head is too small," she said.

"It doesn't need a big head," said Mackenzie. "It has a pea for a brain."

Mackenzie put a peppercorn on each side of the dinosaur's head to make the eyes. After that he was finished.

"You should have made two dinosaurs," said Katie. "For company."

Mackenzie shook his head. "There's not enough plasticine for two. Anyway," he said, "it's getting extinct."

Mackenzie took George out of Katie's backpack. He made George lurk through the leaves in the shoebox and climb up on the back of the dinosaur. "Now the dinosaur's got company," he said.

Katie and Mackenzie left George and the dinosaur in the shoebox on the table. They switched off the light and went up to bed.

George
Travels Back in Time

George was tired. The lessons had made him sleepy. When he woke up he saw danger!

He was in the forest primeval. Big green leaves rustled around him. The air smelled like salt and pepper. In the distance he heard water.

Drip. Drip. Drip.

And right in front of him was a brontosaurus!

Where had the time gone? He had gone back to a time before plastic. He had gone back to a time before books. He had almost gone right past the beginning of the world. Right out of time.

Out of time! Out of time!

It was a good thing George woke up before that.

The dinosaur was munching on a bed of leaves. It had legs as big as tree trunks. George knew he couldn't waste any more time. He hauled himself up the creature's tail. He gripped the dinosaur's belly with his shiny red shoes. He hung on for dear life.

The world went black.

But George hung on. He would stay on the dinosaur's back. He would discover the answer to the biggest secret ever. He would find out what happened to all those dinosaurs!

Katie and Mackenzie and the Dragon Rocket

Katie and Mackenzie were buying fireworks at the fireworks trailer. They bought some black snakes, a silver fountain, a howler, three repeaters, a Roman candle and a package of sparklers. After counting their money they bought a burning schoolhouse too.

You can't do fireworks and not have a burning schoolhouse.

When they went to pay, Mackenzie saw a box with one small yellow rocket. Green dragons were painted around the sides, green dragons with orange eyes and long black tongues. The bottom of the rocket was covered in red streamers.

The advertisement said, "Goes higher than a Roman candle. Explodes into ten thousand white lights. Inside that are one thousand red lights. Inside that are one hundred green lights."

"Wow!" said Mackenzie. "I want this one."

Katie said, "We don't have enough money. You have to put another one back."

So Mackenzie put the silver fountain back.

That night they saved the yellow rocket for last. Usually people save the burning schoolhouse for last. Then they do the sparklers. But Katie and Mackenzie wanted to make the rocket the last.

Just before they lit the rocket they tied George to the side.

Maybe this was Mackenzie's idea. Maybe it was Katie's idea. It doesn't matter. When their mom lit the firework, she didn't see the little guy. The rocket blasted into the sky. And George went too.

George
in Space

George shook himself awake. He was ready for his mission. He had discovered history. Now he would make it!

He climbed onto the rocket. He checked his seatbelt. Above him the night sky twinkled like a deep dish of blackberry syrup. He counted down. Ten, nine … The engines began to burn.

Six, five … The flame turned into a hot white light.

Three, two, one … The world began to shimmy and shake.

Blastoff!

George was on the frontier of space! He was

getting closer and closer to the stars. He was getting so close the stars turned into lightbulbs.

The lights on earth shrank. They were so far away they turned into pinpricks.

The rocket kept on going straight up. The air got colder and colder. The jets got hotter and hotter. Maybe he would not stop at the moon. He would steer the rocket past Mars. He would go right through the rings of Saturn. After Pluto he would thumb a ride on a comet and hitchhike to the stars!

Suddenly the jets of the rocket went out. For a moment all George could hear was the icy silence of space.

Boom! Ten thousand lights exploded around him.

Boom!

Boom!

Boom!

He had reached the Milky Way! He was on the highway of the stars.

Boom! The lights turned red. Stop!

Boom! The lights turned green. Go!

It was a traffic jam. A traffic jam so big it was out of this world!

George couldn't decide what to do. One arm wanted to go one way. The other arm wanted to go another way. And the legs wouldn't follow each other.

It was every part for itself!

Katie and Mackenzie
"Oh-oh!"

The red rocket burst into ten thousand bright lights. The red ones came next. The green ones lasted the longest. They drew wavy lines when they fell from the sky.

Katie and Mackenzie stood in the backyard. They closed their eyes and watched the fireworks all over again in their eyeballs.

Thump! Something landed nearby.

"That's George," Katie cried.

They searched in the dark for the little guy. Mackenzie went into the house. He brought back his new flashlight, a shiny blue one with a metal clip. Finally the light picked out a spot of red on the grass.

"There he is!" he yelled.

They bent down to look.

"Oh- oh," said Katie.

"Oh,-oh," said Mackenzie.

All they saw was a red plastic leg and a shiny red shoe.

George?

George lived inside his head. He had his eyes. He had his ears. He would keep them open.

He was George the Brave, George the Steadfast. He would find himself!

Coming soon!

Part Two:
George Most Wanted

Will George find all his parts?

Ingrid Lee's unusual imagination is just as comfortable carrying her into the head of a small plastic toy, a dragon sand-sculpture or an ordinary girl or boy. She lives in Toronto, Ontario, and *The True Story of George* is her first book.